Muck
and the Machine Convoy

Illustrations by Jerry Smith
Cover illustration by Craig Cameron

EGMONT

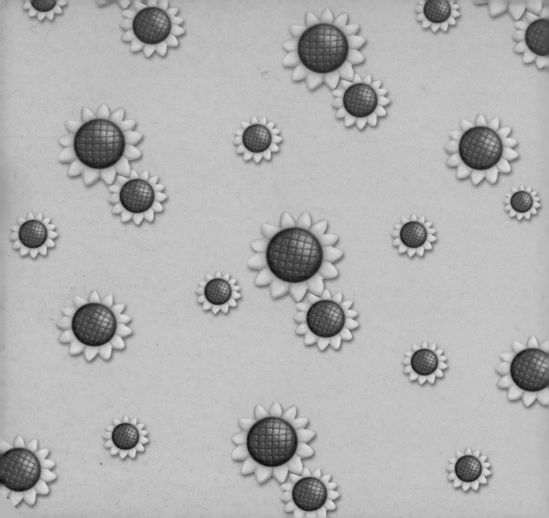

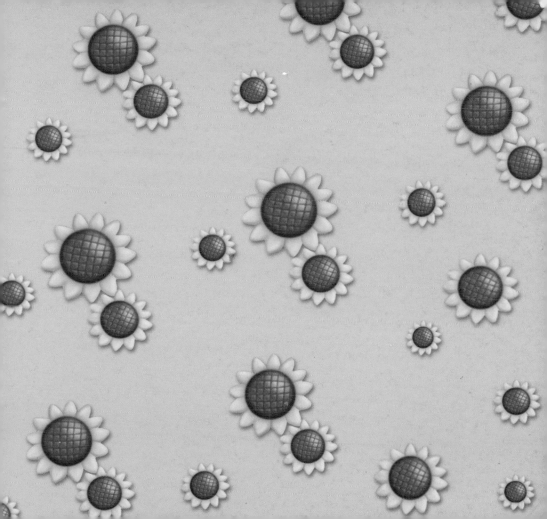

EGMONT
We bring stories to life

First published in Great Britain 2008 by Egmont UK Limited
The Yellow Building,1 Nicholas Road, London W11 4AN

Endpapers and introductory illustrations by Craig Cameron.

HiT entertainment

ISBN 978 1 4052 3749 9

45329/4

Printed in Italy

FSC
www.fsc.org
MIX
Paper from
responsible sources
FSC® C018306

Egmont is passionate about helping to preserve the world's remaining ancient forests.
We only use paper from legal and sustainable forest sources.

This book is made from paper certified by the Forest Stewardship Council® (FSC®),
an organisation dedicated to promoting responsible management of forest resources.
For more information on the FSC, please visit www.fsc.org. To learn more about
Egmont's sustainable paper policy, please visit www.egmont.co.uk/ethical

The Old Watermill
needs a new waterwheel.
Muck is given the job
of leader, but can he
lead the machines
safely to the mill?

Bob and the team were going to build a waterwheel for the Old Watermill.

"How will it work?" wondered Scoop.

Bob explained that the flow of the river fills the buckets, which push the waterwheel round. The wheel turns the cogs inside the mill. Then, the cogs turn big stones that rub together and crush the grain into flour.

"Water power! Cool!" said Muck.

"We have to take the waterwheel to the mill," said Bob. "It comes apart, so we can take it in pieces."

Bob climbed up the ladder and loosened some nuts and screws. Lofty carefully put the pieces in Muck's tipper and Scoop's scoop, and the final part on to Benny's forklift.

The parts were heavy. It was going to be a bumpy ride!

"Muck, you will be in charge of the convoy," said Bob.

"Erm . . . Bob, what's a convoy?" he asked.

"It's when a group of machines follow each other in a line," Bob said. "You will be the leader because you can flatten a path with your caterpillar tracks for the others to follow."

Muck's new job made him feel special. He didn't want to make any mistakes.

Bob told Muck how to get to the Old Watermill. "But remember," he said, "don't go into the marshland, or you'll get stuck."

"Can Muck lead us?" said Scoop.

"Yes, he can," called the team.

"Er, yeah. I hope so," worried Lofty.

"You can rely on Muck! Convoy – follow me!" said Muck, whizzing ahead. Benny, Scoop and Lofty rolled along behind him.

Bob, Travis and Dizzy took a short cut to take the scaffolding to the mill, where Wendy was waiting. The convoy was doing well.

On the way they saw a line of ducks waddle across the track. "Oh, hello, duckies. You're in a convoy just like us!" chuckled Muck.

But there was no time to stop and talk, so Muck and the team hurried on.

Meanwhile, at the Old Watermill, Bob and Wendy had almost finished the scaffolding.

"I wonder what's taking Muck so long?" thought Bob. "I'll call him on the talkie-talkie," he said. "Bob to Muck. How are you doing? Over."

"Umm . . . hello, Bob. We're doing . . . really well," said Muck, quietly.

"Great. See you soon. Over," said Bob.

But Muck and the convoy weren't doing well, at all. "Are you sure you went the right way, Muck?" asked Lofty.

"Quiet, please. Your leader needs to think!" huffed Muck, and rolled along bravely. But he was soon feeling glum.

"Oh, no! We're right back where we started!" moaned Benny.

The convoy was back at the yard!

By now, Muck and the convoy were feeling very tired.

Finally, they reached the river. "Well done, Muck! We're nearly there!" cheered Lofty.

"I did it! Let's cut across the marsh. It'll be quicker," said Muck, rolling down the riverbank.

But the convoy didn't follow at once. "I'm sure Muck knows what he's doing," urged Scoop. "Follow the leader!"

Schlup . . . schlup . . . schlup went their wheels through the muddy marsh.

Poor Lofty, his wheels had sunk deep into the mud. "You said you wouldn't get me stuck, Muck!" he bawled.

"This is all my fault. Leaders shouldn't make mistakes," worried Muck.

The ducklings were crossing the marsh, too. But one was stuck, like Lofty. The mother duck gave it a push, and the duckling waddled free.

Watching the ducks gave Lofty an idea.

He pushed Lofty with all his might. Slowly, Lofty eased out of the marsh and on to the track.

"Someone else should be leader. I've made too many mistakes," sighed Muck.

"Bob always says good leaders are ones who make a mistake and then put it right. And you did just that!" said Scoop, kindly.

The team got back in line, ready for Muck to lead them to the Watermill.

Finally, Muck's convoy arrived at the mill. "I'm sorry, Bob," mumbled Muck. "We went in a big circle . . . and got lost. Then Lofty got stuck in the marsh . . ."

"Muck did a brilliant job leading us here," said Scoop.

"Yeah, he was like unreal banana peel!" joined in Benny.

"Well done, Muck," cheered Bob. Muck beamed happily with everyone's praise.

"Now, let's finish building the waterwheel," said Bob. With all the team helping, it was soon complete. Bob turned the handle outside, and slowly, the waterwheel began to turn.

"Hooray!" cheered the team.

Just then, the mother duck and her ducklings floated past on the river.

"Looks like we both got our convoys here safely!" Muck said, proudly.

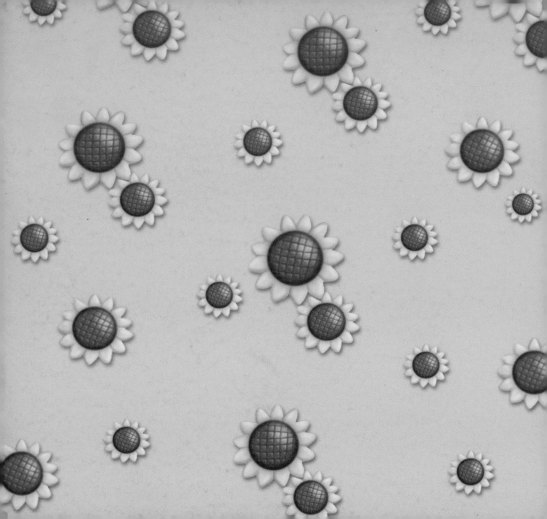